The
Ghost
on the
Hearth

For information about permission to reproduce selections from this book, write to

PERMISSIONS
THE VERMONT FOLKLIFE CENTER
MASONIC HALL
3 COURT STREET, BOX 442
MIDDLEBURY, VERMONT 05753

LIBRARY OF CONGRESS | CATALOGING-IN-PUBLICATION DATA

Milord, Susan.
    The ghost on the hearth / retold by Susan Milord; paintings by Lydia Dabcovich.
        p. cm. – (The family heritage series)
    Summary: In rural Quebec in the 1830s, Jenny is hired to help a family by cooking
 and cleaning after her predecessor, the beloved Emily, has died, but Jenny is
 mysteriously prevented from completing one of her chores.
    ISBN 0-916718-18-2
    [1. Household employees–Fiction. 2. Ghosts–Fiction. 3. Farm life–Canada–Fiction.
 4. Ontario–History–1791-1841–Fiction. 5. Canada–History–1763-1867–Fiction.]
 I. Dabcovich, Lydia, ill. II. Title. III. Series.

    PZ7.M6445 Gh 2003
    [Fic]–dc21

                                                    2003024004

ISBN 0-916718-18-2
Printed in China

First Edition

Book design: Joseph Lee, Black Fish Design
Series Editor: William Jaspersohn

10 9 8 7 6 5 4 3 2 1

Publication of this book was made possible by grants from the Walter Cerf
Community Fund and the Christian A. Johnson Endeavor Foundation.

A Vermont Folklife Center Book

The Ghost on the Hearth

RETOLD BY
SUSAN MILORD

PAINTINGS BY
LYDIA DABCOVICH

DISTRIBUTED BY UNIVERSITY PRESS OF NEW ENGLAND
HANOVER AND LONDON

In a small town in rural Quebec there once lived a poor man and his wife and their nine children. The eldest was a girl named Emily.

In those days, children from poor families were often sent to live with farm families that were a little better off. This took some of the burden off a family where there were a lot of children, besides giving farmers more hands to lighten their work.

Emily was such a girl. In the summer of her twelfth
year, she left home to live on a farm just outside of town.

In exchange for room and board, she
helped the farmer's wife cook, clean, and sew.
Each morning when she rose, she started
a fire in the big wood stove in the kitchen.

Before she went to sleep each evening, she
scraped the wax drippings from the great stone hearth.

Emily was a pleasant girl with a generous heart and a ready smile. The farmer and his wife grew to love her, much as they did their own children. When the girl fell ill one winter, they sent for the doctor and took turns keeping watch at her bedside. When she grew worse, they sent for the girl's parents and brothers and sisters.

"I'm afraid there's nothing more we can do for your Emily," the doctor told them. "She's in God's hands now."

The two families gathered by Emily's side, their heads bowed in prayer. As the evening sun sank behind the hills, the frail girl drew her last breath and died.

Not long after, another young girl came to live and work at the farm. Like Emily before her, Jenny's duties included cooking, cleaning, and scraping the hardened wax from the hearthstone each evening.

One morning, the farmer's wife was surprised to see there was wax on the hearthstone. She went into the garden, where she found Jenny picking vegetables for the midday meal.

"It's important that you scrape the wax from the hearthstone each night," she said to the girl.

Jenny looked puzzled. "I did clean it, ma'am," she said.

"Perhaps you'd better come and see," the farmer's wife replied.

Jenny's face reddened when she saw the hardened wax on the great stone slab. "I know you don't believe me," she said, "but I did clean the hearth before I went to bed last night. I remember it very well. The clock chimed eight just as I was finishing up."

"I want to believe you, Jenny, I really do. But why is there wax on the hearth now if you removed it last night?" asked the farmer's wife.

"I don't know," replied Jenny.

The farmer's wife told her husband about Jenny and the wax. That evening, he watched as the girl cleaned the fresh drippings. Satisfied that it had been done, he told his wife to put the incident behind her.

The next morning, however, they discovered several small fresh patches of melted wax on the hearth.

"But I saw Jenny clean the stone last night with my own eyes," insisted the farmer.

"Then how do you explain the wax?" his wife asked.

"I cannot," the farmer replied.

"Someone's bent on making mischief," the farmer declared, "but who can it be? I guess there's nothing to do but keep watch."

That night, he made himself comfortable in the rocking chair in the parlor. But the steady tick tock tick tock of the grandfather clock made his eyelids droop, and before long he was fast asleep. He woke early that morning, only to find fresh wax on the hearth.

"I'll stay up and watch tonight," the farmer's wife offered. "Maybe I'll have better luck."

When the others had gone to bed, she gathered up her knitting and sat by the fire. "Knit one, purl one, knit one, purl one . . . ," she repeated aloud to herself. "Slip one, knit two together," she chanted. Her needles clacked as she worked her way from one end of a sleeve to the other. But even her steady chatter could not keep her awake, and before long the farmer's wife fell fast asleep.

Suddenly, the farmer's wife woke with a start. The hair on the back of her neck bristled. She had the uncomfortable feeling that she wasn't alone in the room.

As her eyes adjusted to the dark, the woman could just make out the ghostly figure of a girl, illuminated by the faint glow of candlelight.

"Emily! Is that you?" the farmer's wife gasped.

The ghostly girl turned toward the farmer's wife, her head bowed. "It is," she said. "I beg of you, please do not be angry with me."

"Angry?" asked the farmer's wife. "Whatever for?"

"For returning to your house as a ghost," Emily replied. "And for burning these candles."

The farmer's wife smiled. "So it was you!" she said. "But why, Emily, why have you been burning candles?"

Emily lowered her eyes. "As punishment," she said simply.

"I don't understand" the farmer's wife replied. "Punishment . . . for what?"

"When I worked for you," Emily began, "I took the stubs of the candles each night to give to my own family. It was wrong, I know it was, but we never had enough candles in my family's house."

The girl paused. "When I died, I was condemned to burn as many candles as I took home."

"Oh, Emily," the farmer's wife said gently, "had I known that your family needed candles, I would have been happy to give them some. You mustn't be punished for trying to help your family. All is forgiven. Go in peace, dear child, go in peace."

After that, the farmer and his wife never had
another encounter with Emily's ghost. Nor did they
ever find candle wax on the hearth again.

In the Mood

WHEN CLAIRE CHASE WAS A LITTLE GIRL GROWING UP IN Winooski, Vermont, storytelling was a regular part of her daily life. Her parents would tell her bedtime stories they had heard as children, and on holidays, such as Christmas or New Year's, the family would gather after supper around the potbelly stove, and Claire's grandparents would tell scary stories, fantastical legends, and tales of the supernatural. To set the mood for the storytelling session, all the electric lights would be turned off. The only illumination came from the stove's window or from a candle on the kitchen table.

You, your family, and friends can set the mood for your own scary storytelling sessions the same way Claire's family did—by turning down the lights. Good times for such sessions are holidays with relatives, slumber parties with friends, overnight camp-outs—even nighttime gatherings on the family front porch.

Here are three ideas to get your story started:

1. Tell a scary story that you've read, heard, or seen. Maybe it's a favorite book or movie, or a story that's been passed down in your family for generations.
2. Tell a true story from your own experience about something that really frightened you.
3. Make up your own scary story using "story starter" ideas suggested by the group. Story starters are characters, objects, settings, and situations that can fire your imagination. Some storytellers write such ideas on index cards and store them in recipe boxes. When they need inspiration, they sift through their cards, find an idea and—whammo!—a story always comes to them.

To create your own story-starter box, you'll need:

Index Cards
Pen or Pencil
Recipe Box
Ideas for Characters, Objects, Settings, and Situations
   1. Ask your friends and family for ideas.
   2. Jot the ideas down on the cards.
   3. Pull out your box the next time you're all in a storytelling mood!

Examples

Character: An Evil Troll
Character: A Talking Deer
Character: An Orphan Girl Named (blank)
Character: A Boy Lost in the Woods
Character: An Old Woman with a Glass Eye
Characters: Three Schoolgirls
Character: A Pirate Captain
Object: A Magic Canoe
Object: A Magic Tooth
Object: A Witch's Whisker
Object: A Talking Doll
Object: An Evil Pair of Shoes
Setting: A Dark, Enchanted Woods
Setting: A Haunted Schoolhouse
Setting: A Cave Near the Ocean
Setting: A Barren Desert
Setting: An Old Volcano
Situation: You are walking to school one morning when suddenly a hole opens in the ground, and a creaky voice says, "Come in, my child...."
Situation: One day you are in math class when you notice something slimy and whiplike sprouting from a classmate's head.
Situation: Your dog casts a spell, turning you into a dog and himself into a human being.
Situation: Every morning when you wake up, there is a gold coin in your cereal bowl.
Situation: Something in the woods is leaving giant, apelike footprints! You vow to find out what.